THE ANT AND THE GRASSHOPPER

Why should you prepare for tomorrow?

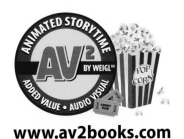

www.av2books.com

Go to **www.av2books.com**, and enter this book's unique code.

BOOK CODE

C154229

AV² by Weigl brings you media enhanced books that support active learning.

Published by AV² by Weigl
350 5th Avenue, 59th Floor New York, NY 10118

Library of Congress Cataloging-in-Publication Data

The ant and the grasshopper.
   p. cm. -- (Aesop's fables by AV2)
 Summary: The familiar Aesop fable is performed by a troupe of animal actors.
 ISBN 978-1-61913-106-4 (hard cover : alk. paper)
[1. Fables. 2. Folklore.] I. Aesop.
 PZ8.2.A6 2012
 398.2--dc23
 [E]
                              2012018616

Printed in the United States in North Mankato, Minnesota
1 2 3 4 5 6 7 8 9 0   16 15 14 13 12

052012
WEP290512

FABLE SYNOPSIS

For thousands of years, parents and teachers have used memorable stories called fables to teach simple moral lessons to children.

In the Aesop's Fables by AV² series, classic fables are given a lighthearted twist. These familiar tales are performed by a troupe of animal players whose endearing personalities bring the stories to life.

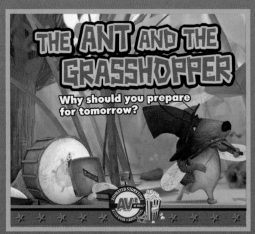

In *The Ant and the Grasshopper*, Aesop teaches his troupe about the importance of hard work. They learn to prepare today for what they will need tomorrow.

This AV² media enhanced book comes alive with...

 Animated Video
Watch a custom animated movie.

 Try This!
Complete activities and hands on experiments.

 Key Words
Study vocabulary and hands-on experiments.

 Quiz
Test your knowledge.

THE ANT AND THE GRASSHOPPER

Why should you prepare for tomorrow?

AV² Storytime Navigation

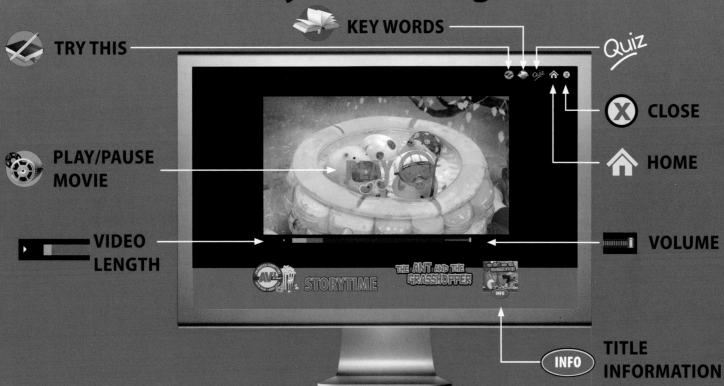

KEY WORDS

TRY THIS

Quiz

X CLOSE

PLAY/PAUSE MOVIE

HOME

VIDEO LENGTH

VOLUME

INFO — **TITLE INFORMATION**

The Players

Aesop
I am the leader of Aesop's Theater, a screenwriter, and an actor.
I can be hot-tempered, but I am also soft and warm-hearted.

Libbit
I am an actor and a prop man.
I think I should have been a lion, but I was born a rabbit.

Presy
I am the manager of Aesop's Theater.
I am also the narrator of the plays.

The Story

One summer day, Aesop was writing a play.

There were crumpled sheets of paper all over the floor.

Libbit was singing into a fan.

"What are you doing?" asked Aesop.

"I'm singing a song! The fan makes my voice sound funny."

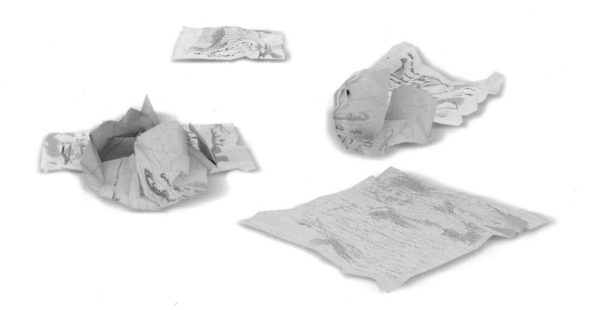

"I'm trying to work. Get out!" shouted Aesop.

"But it's too hot outside," said Libbit.

"I can not write with the noise you're making," replied Aesop.

Aesop opened the refrigerator.

"Where is the water and ice?"

"The Shorties took it outside."

Aesop left the house.

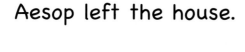

The Shorties were playing in the pool.

Blocks of ice were floating in the water.

"You five took my ice and drinking water!"

Aesop was mad at the Shorties.

"I'm trying to work even though it is hot,

and you're just playing in the water!"

The Shorties just stared at Aesop.

13

Presy was sitting in the shade with her feet off the ground.

"You write too much Aesop! You should take a break with me."

Aesop was disappointed by what she said.

"Maybe we can all learn something from my new play."

16

Aesop gathered everyone together.

"My new play is called *The Ant and the Grasshopper*,

I hope you will learn something by acting in my play."

The Shorties will play the hard-working ants,

and Aesop will play the grasshopper.

A group of ants were working hard on a hot day.

Suddenly, they heard someone playing the violin.

It was the grasshopper! Two ants saw him under a big tree.

He was the musician of the forest.

The grasshopper danced to his music in the shade.

"Hello ants! Would you like to play with me?"

"Sorry, we must store up food for winter."

"But it's summer. You have lots of time."

The ants kept working.

The grasshopper laughed at the ants.

"I will have a good time playing on my own."

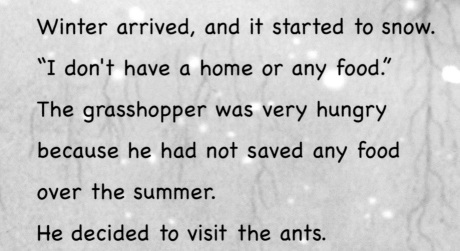

Winter arrived, and it started to snow.

"I don't have a home or any food."

The grasshopper was very hungry

because he had not saved any food

over the summer.

He decided to visit the ants.

The grasshopper knocked on their door.

"Would you give me something to eat?"
asked the grasshopper.

"You were foolish enough to sing all
summer, and now you must dance
to bed hungry," said the ants.

The disappointed grasshopper
said goodbye and left.

When the play was finished, Aesop
returned to his writing.
The Shorties arrived and started to
practice and make a fuss.
Libbit and Presy arrived,
and helped the pigs.
They all learned their lesson and kept
Aesop awake until late that night.

By preparing today, they will be
ready for what they need tomorrow.

What is a Story?

Players

Who is the story about? The characters, or players, are the people, animals, or objects that perform the story. Characters have personality traits that contribute to the story. Readers understand how a character fits into the story by what the character says and does, what others say about the character, and how others treat the character.

Setting

Where and when do the events take place? The setting of a story helps readers visualize where and when the story is taking place. These details help to suggest the mood or atmosphere of the story. A setting is usually presented briefly, but it explains whether the story is taking place in the past, present, or future and in a large or small area.

Plot

What happens in the story? The plot is a story's plan of action. Most plots follow a pattern. They begin with an introduction and progress to the rising action of events. The events lead to a climax, which is the most exciting moment in the story. The resolution is the falling action of events. This section ties up loose ends so that readers are not left with unanswered questions. The story ends with a conclusion that brings the events to a close.

Point of View

Who is telling the story? The story is normally told from the point of view of the narrator, or storyteller. The narrator can be a main character or a less important character in the story. He or she can also be someone who is not in the story but is observing the action. This observer may be impartial or someone who knows the thoughts and feelings of the characters. A story can also be told from different points of view.

Dialogue

What type of conversation occurs in the story? Conversation, or dialogue, helps to show what is happening. It also gives information about the characters. The reader can discover what kinds of people they are by the words they say and how they say them. Writers use dialogue to make stories more interesting. In dialogue, writers imitate the way real people speak, so it is written differently than the rest of the story.

Theme

What is the story's underlying meaning? The theme of a story is the topic, idea, or position that the story presents. It is often a general statement about life. Sometimes, the theme is stated clearly. Other times, it is suggested through hints.

THE ANT AND THE GRASSHOPPER Quiz

1
Who was singing into the fan?

2
Who took the water and ice?

3
Why was Aesop mad at the shorties?

4
What instrument was the grasshopper playing?

5
Why was the grasshopper hungry?

6
What did the players learn?

Key Words

Research has shown that as much as 65 percent of all written material published in English is made up of 300 words. These 300 words cannot be taught using pictures or learned by sounding them out. They must be recognized by sight. This book contains 114 common sight words to help young readers improve their reading fluency and comprehension. This book also teaches young readers several important content words, such as proper nouns. These words are paired with pictures to aid in learning and improve understanding.

Page	Sight Words First Appearance
4	a, also, am, an, and, be, been, but, can, have, I, of, plays, should, the, think, was
5	always, animals, at, do, food, from, get, good, if, like, never, other, them, to, very, want, with
7	all, are, asked, day, into, makes, my, one, over, paper, song, sound, there, were, what, you
9	house, is, it, it's, left, not, out, said, too, took, water, where, work, write
10	in
12	even, just
15	by, feet, learn, me, much, new, off, she, something, take, we
17	will
19	big, group, hard, he, him, his, on, saw, they, tree, two, under
21	for, must, own, time, up, would
23	any, because, don't, had, home, or, started
25	eat, enough, give, now, their
27	need, night, that, until, when

Page	Content Words First Appearance
4	actor, leader, lion, manager, narrator, prop man, rabbit, screenwriter, theater
5	dance, music, pig
7	fan, floor, voice
9	ice, noise, noise, refrigerator
10	pool
15	ground, shade
17	ant, grasshopper
19	violin
21	winter, summer
25	bed, door

Check out av2books.com for your animated storytime media enhanced book!

1. Go to av2books.com
2. Enter book code C154229
3. Fuel your imagination online!

www.av2books.com

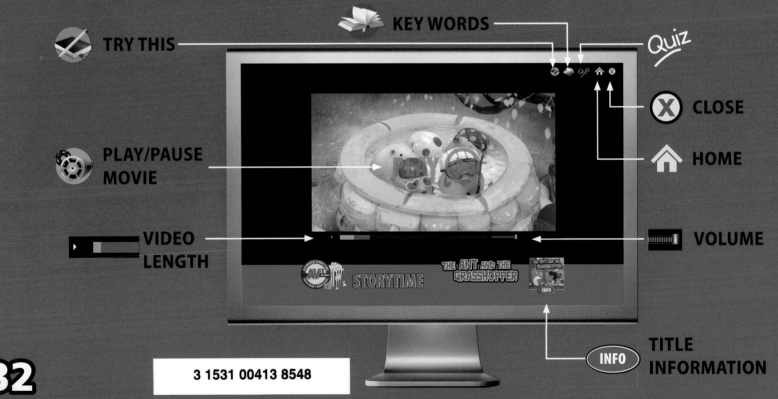

AV² Storytime Navigation

KEY WORDS

Quiz

TRY THIS

CLOSE

PLAY/PAUSE MOVIE

HOME

VIDEO LENGTH

VOLUME

INFO — TITLE INFORMATION